Runaway Pumpkins

To Grace, Dane, Maggie, and Aria, as well as the students at Olympic View Elementary who lost their pumpkins.—T. B.

For Seth and all our pumpkin-carving adventures!—S. F. C.

Published by Charlesbridge
85 Main Street, Watertown, MA 02472
(617) 926–0329 • www.charlesbridge.com

Printed in China
(hc) 10 9 8 7 6 5 4 3 2 1

Illustrations done digitally
Display type hand-lettered by Stephanie Fizer Coleman
Text type set in Baileywick JF by Jason Anthony Walcott
    and Helenita by Rodrigo Typo
Color separations by Colourscan Print Co Pte LTD, Singapore
Printed by 1010 Printing International Limited in Huizhou,
    Guangdong, China
Production supervision by Brian G. Walker
Designed by Joyce White and Sarah Richards Taylor

Library of Congress Cataloging-in-Publication Data
Names: Bateman, Teresa, author. | Coleman, Stephanie Fizer, illustrator.
Title: Runaway pumpkins / Teresa Bateman; illustrated by Stephanie Fizer Coleman.
Description: Watertown, MA: Charlesbridge, [2020] | Summary: When a poorly secured bus lock turns
    a school trip back from a pumpkin patch into a disaster, and all but one of the pumpkins end up
    in people's yards, the neighbors along the road come up with a plan to turn the pumpkins into
    treats for the school children.
Identifiers: LCCN 2018025048 (print) | LCCN 2018032445 (ebook) | ISBN 9781632898241 (ebook) |
    ISBN 9781632898258 (ebook pdf) | ISBN 9781580896818 (reinforced for library use)
Subjects: LCSH: Pumpkin—Juvenile fiction. | School field trips—Juvenile fiction. | Stories in rhyme. |
    CYAC: Stories in rhyme. | Pumpkin—Fiction. | School field trips—Fiction. | LCGFT: Stories in rhyme.
Classification: LCC PZ8.3.B314 (ebook) | LCC PZ8.3.B314 Ru 2018 (print) |
    DDC 813.54 [E]—dc23
LC record available at https://lccn.loc.gov/2018025048

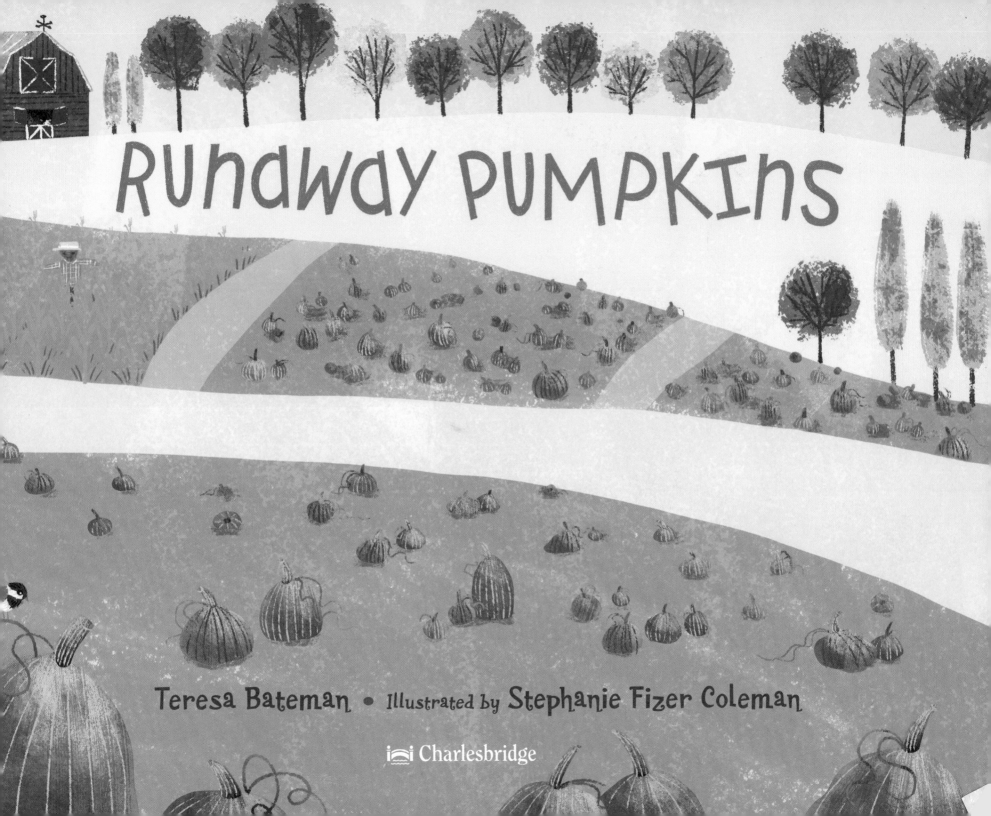

Runaway Pumpkins

Teresa Bateman • Illustrated by Stephanie Fizer Coleman

Charlesbridge

Leaves are twirling to the ground.
Teachers call out all around,
"Grab your lunch—the bus is here!"
Everybody gives a cheer.

"Load 'em up!" the driver calls.
Students flow from tiled halls.
Thump, thump, thump in merry pairs—
tennis shoes on metal stairs.

Windows fog as faces grin.

The field trip's ready to begin.

Doors swing closed and hatches latch.

Bump, bump, bump to the pumpkin patch.

Driving through the countryside,
everyone enjoys the ride.
Children chuckle—chitter-chatter—
noisy, but it doesn't matter.

"Picking pumpkins!"

"We'll have fun!"

"Why can't I choose
more than one?"

At the farm, doors open wide.
All the children rush outside.
Students run and point and call.
It's turned into a free-for-all!

Pumpkins big and pumpkins tiny.
Short and fat,
and dull and shiny.
Bumpy, lumpy,
straight or curvy.
Really round
or topsy-turvy.

PICK YOUR OWN

Children dash by, laughing, quick.

This one, that one—

which to pick?

At last each student
finds the one—
the perfect pumpkin.
Searching's done!

Wave to pigs out in the sty.

Time to tell the cows goodbye.

Loading up, they shove and wiggle.
Children tease and joke and giggle.
Everybody says, "Hooray!"
What a prodigious pumpkin day!

Eyes are shining. Smiles gleam.
Each student has a pumpkin dream
of funny, weird, or scary faces—
even ears in funny places.

Going back to school, aglow.
Plans are bubbling,
but . . . OH, NO!

Latches holding hatches tight
were almost fastened,
but not quite.

Pumpkins here, pumpkins there,
pumpkins rolling everywhere.
Leaping lawn gnomes,
striking stairs,
charging into wicker chairs.

When, at last, they come to rest,
they're bruised and busted—
what a mess!

Neighbors see the big snafu.
The bus is gone.
Now what to do?

"These pumpkins found
our cul-de-sac.
What if the children want them back?"

The neighbors come up with a plan
to do the very best they can.

They gather pumpkins, all a-tizzy,
take them home, and then get busy.

Back at school, cries of woe.

"Where did all our pumpkins go?"

"I wish I knew." A teacher sighs.

"I'm sorry for this sad surprise."

The children slump in misery.

Then Kim perks up. "Just look and see—

a single pumpkin's on the bus.

It's big enough for all of us!"

The children come up with a plan
to do the very best they can.

They get out paper, paints, and glue.
Each student has a job to do.
Talking, laughing—everyone
is joining in and having fun.

The next day is the harvest fair,
and look who's here, with food to share!
The neighbors in a big parade
bring all the pumpkin foods they made.

There's pumpkin soup
and pumpkin pie.
Pumpkin cake.
Pumpkin fries!
Pumpkin ice cream,
cookies too.
And is that pumpkin barbecue?

The students rejoice. What a happy surprise.

"Our pumpkins are back, but they came in disguise!"

Everyone sits while they pass round the treats,
and students and neighbors all grin as they eat.

Yet one smile is wider than all the rest.
It's the one on the face
of their most honored guest.

Make some pumpkin treats of your own!
Always get help from a grown-up before using the oven or baking.

CARAMEL FROSTED PUMPKIN COOKIES

Prep time: 25 minutes | Yield: About 4 dozen | Preheat oven to 375° F

COOKIES

4 cups flour
2 tsp baking soda
1 tsp ground cinnamon
1 tsp salt
2 cups butter or margarine
2 cups granulated sugar
2 cups (16 oz) cooked or canned pumpkin
2 eggs

Combine dry ingredients in a bowl and stir until mixed well, then set aside. In a different bowl, cream the butter, sugar, and pumpkin together with an electric mixer (or by hand with a wooden spoon). Add eggs and mix well. Gradually add the dry ingredients and stir until everything is mixed together. Spoon dollops onto an ungreased cookie sheet. Bake for 10 to 12 minutes at 375° F. Frost while warm.

CARAMEL FROSTING

6 tbsp butter
8 tsp milk
1 cup brown sugar
2 cups powdered sugar
1 tsp vanilla

Combine butter, milk, and brown sugar in a saucepan. Heat on low until sugar dissolves, then remove from heat and let cool. Stir in the powdered sugar and vanilla until smooth. Frost cookies.

NOTE: Don't put these cookies into a sealed container, because they'll get soggy. If you keep them out, they'll stay crispy around the edges.